Hippety-hop, Hippety-hay

Growing with rhymes from birth to age 3

Opal Dunn

Illustrated by
Sally Anne Lambert

FRANCES LINCOLN

Contents

For Lily and Michael ~ O. D.

*For my children, Jonny and Katie
and my Mum and Dad,
with all my love ~ S. A. L.*

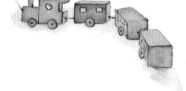

Hippety-hop, Hippety-hay copyright © Frances Lincoln Limited 1999
Text copyright © Opal Dunn 1999
Illustrations copyright © Sally Anne Lambert 1999

First published in Great Britain in 1999 by Frances Lincoln Limited,
4 Torriano Mews, Torriano Avenue, London NW5 2RZ

British Library Cataloguing in Publication Data
available on request

ISBN 0-7112-1327-5

Set in Stone Serif and Stone Sans

Printed in Hong Kong
Repro by Evergreen Colour Separation (Int'l) Co Ltd.

9 8 7 6 5 4 3 2 1

Dear Parents and Carers,

Have you ever stopped to think how, where and when your baby learns to talk, or who teaches her? Her teacher is you! As you go about caring for her everyday physical needs, you talk to her. It's from your speech that she picks up language. The special soft voice you use, and the slow, often repetitive way you speak to her help her learn to talk.

From the moment she is born, she is learning to speak, but she can only learn if she is spoken to and joins in the dialogue. You can give her a head start in understanding and using language. The more you talk with her, the greater her opportunity to learn. The more your toddler develops her language skills, the better she will be able to understand what is going on around her, and learn from it. A child who cannot understand language easily finds learning more difficult.

You may not find it easy to talk to her, especially when she's very tiny, but don't give up. Simple rhymes, like those in this collection, can help you interact with her at a level that matches her development. Try them – you'll find your child responds, even from a few months old.

Each rhyme in this book is included for a reason. They are all ideal for learning and for livening up routine activities. To make understanding simpler for your child, I've matched the rhymes to developmental levels, and divided them into age-related sections. But this is just a guide. Your child, like all children, develops at her own pace. I've suggested actions to go with the rhymes, as she will learn more quickly if she is physically involved with the language.

Throughout the book I have referred to babies and toddlers as "she" but, of course, these rhymes are perfect for boys, too. You'll find it's fun to personalise the rhymes, adding your child's name where you can. There is music for some rhymes at the back of the book, and you may want to make up your own tunes for others. Once you know the rhymes well, try inventing new verses to fit family occasions.

Rhymes are portable playthings. You can use these rhymes any time and any place. The more you say the rhymes together, the quicker their simple, everyday language will become part of your child's life and speech – providing a valuable preparation for learning to read. So start early, and enjoy every minute!

Opal Dunn

2-6 months

At birth your baby is aware of the sound of your voice. You can begin to use soothing, rocking rhymes, and rhymes involving very, very gentle physical contact, as early as you wish. At about 2 months your baby may begin to smile and by 3 months her cooing develops into babbling. She still sleeps for long periods, but daily routines of bathing, changing and feeding provide ideal opportunities for using rhymes. Follow the rhymes with questions, using a soft tone of voice to encourage a response.

Add new rhymes as your baby develops understanding. Show her that words are associated with things (*Cheek, chin*), with actions (*UP baby goes!*), and with routines (*It's time to say, "Good night!"*). Touch and massage (*Round and round it goes*), help to strengthen bonding.

6-12 months

Baby can sit up now, and sees things from a different angle. She can follow adults around the room with her eyes and recognises family names. Gradually, she is discovering how to use her lips to make different sounds, and she enjoys these vocal experiments. Some of the sounds resemble words like "Mama" and "Dada". Baby begins to wave, clap and even point at things. Towards the end of this period she begins to crawl or move in her own fashion, as a preparation for walking, expanding her experience and her view of the world. Now she is eager for more physical involvement and may even be ready to turn the page in a book. She enjoys knee-jogging (*One, two, three*), and appreciates help in learning to turn over (*Grandpa Grigg*). Continue to use the early rhymes during these months, as she will enjoy their familiarity, and introduce the new rhymes, talking to her more and more as her understanding grows.

As you say rhymes, try to:

* speak softly and slowly, stressing important words or phrases.
* place your face close to baby's, so that she can see your eyes and mouth.
* pause before important words – suspense adds fun!
* say rhymes at least twice. Repetition is comforting.
* identify rhymes with pictures in the book.

These are baby's fingers,
These are baby's toes,
This is baby's tummy button,
Round and round it goes.

As you say the last two lines,
gently circle round baby's
tummy button with your finger.

Hush, baby, hush,
Listen, don't cry,
And I will hum
A lullaby.

Hum a soft tune as you rock your baby.

This is the way
You splash with your feet,
Splash with your feet,
Splash with your feet.
This is the way
You splash with your feet.
Splish, splash, SPLOSH!

Music – see page 44

Jeremiah, blow the fire,
Puff, puff, puff.
First you blow it *gently*…
Then you blow it ROUGH.

Blow onto baby's stomach on each "puff" –
and a little longer on "gently".
End with a big, fun blow on "ROUGH".

Cheek, chin, cheek, chin, cheek, chin,
NOSE,
Cheek, chin, cheek, chin, cheek, chin,
TOES,
Cheek, chin, cheek, chin, cheek, chin –
UP baby goes!

Touch baby as you say the rhyme. On the last line,
hold her ankles together, lift her bottom
and slip her nappy underneath.

Good night, Mummy,
Good night, Daddy,
Good night, Michael,
It's time to say, "Good night".

Good night, Grandma,
Good night, Grandpa,
Good night, Baby,
It's time to say, "Good night!"

Music – see page 44

11

Ride a little pony
Down to town,
Better be careful
You don't fall down.

Jog baby up and down on your knees.
On the final "down", let baby slip
a little way between your knees.

Eazy peazy, nice and easy,
Stretch your arms
And bend your kneesy.

Hold baby's hands together, then gently stretch
her arms out sideways, and let them go.
Hold her legs below the knees, gently bend them
up to her chest and let them go.

Mrs Mouse was cooking rice
For her little babies.
She gave some to this little one,
She gave some to this little one,
She gave some to this little one,
She gave some to this little one,
But when she got to *this* little one…
She ran to the shop to get some more.

Make baby's hand into a rice pot – the fingers
are the little mice. Wiggle each finger.
When you get to the thumb, run your fingers
up the arm and into the armpit "to get some more".

Where's your bear?
Over there.

Now, where's bear?
Look, he's there.

Good night, bear.
Go to sleep
In baby's chair.

Move teddy around, to play
a hide-and-seek game.

Hickety, pickety,
Bumblebee,
Can you say your name
To me?

Big toe,
Tall toe,
Middle toe strong,
Funny toe,
Little toe,
Bongity, bong, BONG.

*Wiggle each toe in turn.
Then clap your hands lightly
against the sole of baby's foot
on "Bongity, bong, BONG".*

Up in the air,
Ever so high,
Grandpa can make
Baby fly.

Ickle, ockle, blue bockle,
Fishes in the sea.
If you want a lovely baby,
Please choose me.

*As you say the rhyme, gently tap baby.
On "me", pick her up and cuddle her.*

Bumblebee came out of the barn,
Carrying bagpipes under his arm,
And went like this – *Buzzzzzzzzz.*

*Circle your finger round and round,
coming closer and closer to your baby,
ready to tickle on Buzzzzzzzzz.*

One, two, three
Baby's on my knee,
Cockerel crows – *Cock-a-doodle-doo!*
And away she goes.

*Bounce baby on your knee.
On the last line, lift baby
high into the air.*

Grandpa Grigg
Had a pig,
In a field of clover.
Piggy died,
Grandpa cried,
And all the fun was OVER.

*Tap baby gently as you
say the rhyme. On "OVER",
help baby to roll over.*

A daisy here,
And a daisy there.
I can see daisies
Everywhere.
Can you?

*Point to the daisies
as you say the rhyme.*

Clap handies, clap handies,
Till Daddy comes home.
Something special
In his pocket
For baby alone.

Knock at the door,
Peep in,
Lift the latch
And walk in.
Chew and swallow –
DOWN it goes.

*Touch baby's forehead lightly, peep into her eyes,
then touch the tip of her nose. On "walk in",
pop the spoon into her mouth.*

Tick, tack, toe,
Round I go,
Where I stop,
I don't know.

Circle your finger round and round.
Touch a part of the body and name it.

Into the buggy
And off we go.
Where are we going?
Do you know?

*Why not say this rhyme as you strap
baby into the buggy or car seat?*

What does the cat say? *Meow*
What does the dog say? *Bow wow*
What does the donkey say? *Hee haw*
What does the bird say? *Caw caw*
What does the cow say? *Mooooo*
What does the farmer say? *Shoo Shoo SHOO*

Gradually add other animals to the rhyme.

Not yet two, I can talk to you

Between 12 and 24 months

During her second year of life, your child's wobbly steps turn into toddling and she runs, dances, jumps and climbs everywhere with great enthusiasm. Her daily routines and experiences expand, naturally broadening the range of your conversations with her. She begins to imitate everything and everybody *(I can laugh* and *Copy me, copy me),* and learns how to communicate with children and adults beyond the immediate family.

Between 12 and 18 months she responds to your talk with single words or phrases, and there are now two of you talking. You still lead the dialogue, but she can converse skilfully using single words such as "cup", to imply, "I am thirsty" and/or "please get me a drink". She can identify things in picture books and may even complete the last word of a line in a rhyme, if you pause and allow her enough time *(Inkey, Winkey, Wonkey* and *One for you and one for me).*

By 18 months your toddler begins to join two words to make phrases like "Dada sit", if she wants her father to sit on a chair. Her vocabulary increases daily. She still understands more words than she can say, and appears to understand most of what is said to her. She finds following simple instructions fun.

Her pronunciation is often cute and immature, but her word order is generally correct, indicating she has already worked out some of the rules of grammar. She copies words and phrases exactly as they are said, and enjoys repeating them back to you. Ask questions beginning with *What?* and *Where?* You will find them especially useful now, allowing you to discover her level of understanding and helping to reinforce the idea that in dialogue speakers take turns.

As you say rhymes, try to:

* continue using a soft voice, stressing important words and using pauses for effect.
* exaggerate your own movements and slow down your speech to match hers.
* position yourself so that she can copy your mouth movements.
* leave out the last word or phrase of a line and use your eyes to indicate that she should complete it. If she isn't ready, quietly do it yourself.
* talk about the illustrations together and let her turn the pages.

I can laugh
And I can cry,
Say, "Hello!"
And wave goodbye.

*As you say the rhyme,
mime the activities.*

Smile a little,
Laugh a little,
Ha, ha, HA!

Say a little,
Sing a little,
La, la, LA!

Little eye – winker,
Little nose – smeller,
Little mouth – eater,
Little chin – chopper,
Chin, chin, chin.

*Wink, sniff, and mime eating.
Touch baby's chin, run your fingers
down her neck, and tickle her.*

UP in the air,
UP in the air,
UP in the air so high,
Way up there,
UP in the air –
What can you see in the sky?

Push the swing as you say each "UP".

Copy me, copy me,
Do just as I do:
Stretch up high,
Reach the sky,
Touch the ground,
Then turn around.

*Your toddler can copy your actions.
Also try: jump up high, dance,
hop, etc.*

Dancing, dancing, jumping up and down.
Dancing, dancing, turning round and round.
Dancing, dancing, falling on the ground!

Most toddlers enjoy falling down –
but make sure they have a safe place to fall.
Music – see page 44

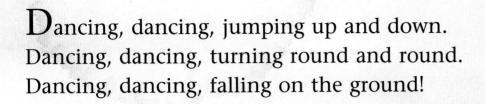

Tickley, tockley, tickley grass,
I can tickle your knee.
Tickley, tockley, tickley grass,
You can't catch me.

Finish by asking your toddler to catch the grass.

Five little ducks went in for a swim,
The first little duck put his head in,
The second little duck put his head back,
The third little duck said, "Quack, quack, quack."
The fourth little duck, with his little brother,
Went for a walk with his father and mother.

As you say the rhyme, wiggle each finger in turn.

Splashing through raindrops,
What did I see?
A wet, brown pussycat
Coming up to me.

Splashing through raindrops,
What did I see?
A big, wet blackbird
Hopping up to me.

Play this game at different times – for example,
"driving in my mummy's car…"

Hippety-hop, hippety-hay,
Five little bunnies went out to play.
Hippety-hippety-hop, hay-hay.
One little bunny ran away.

Four little bunnies…   *(etc.)*

Counting down to:
No little bunnies went out to play
Because they all have run away.
Hippety-hippety-hop, HAY-HAY!

Hold up five fingers and count down.

There were two little birds,
Sat on a stone,
One flew away,
Then there was one.
The other flew after,
Then there were none,
And so the poor stone
Was left all alone.

Use your index fingers to represent the birds.
Then mime the actions.

This is the way you put on your vest,
Put on your vest,
Put on your vest,
This is the way you put on your vest –
Early in the morning.

This is the way you take off your socks,
Take off your socks,
Take off your socks,
This is the way you take off your socks –
It's nearly time for bed.

Make up new verses as you dress and undress your child.
Music – see page 44

 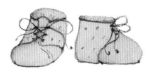

Dan, Dan, the funny wee man,
Washed his face in the frying pan,
Brushed his hair with the leg of a chair,
Dan, Dan, the funny wee man.

When your child is being silly, ask, "Are you Dan?"

Pitter, patter,
Pitter, patter,
What a rainy day!
Let's put on boots,
A raincoat, too,
And go outside to play.

I can be a puffer train,
Puffing down the track.
Now it's going forwards,
Now it's going back.

*Use your body to mime going forwards
and backwards. You can add other actions
or pretend to be other things.*

Fee, fie, foe, fum,
See my fingers,
See my thumb.
Fingers gone –
So is thumb!

*Point to each finger; then wiggle them.
Show the thumb. Make a fist to hide
your fingers, and pop your thumb
into the fist to show "all gone".*

One for you,
And one for me,
And one for everyone
You see.

Tip toe,
Tip toe,
Watch me,
Off I go.
Tip toe,
Tip toe,
Which way
Shall I go?

1 2 3 4 5,
See what I can do.
1 2 3 4 5,
You can say it, too.

*Hold up your fingers as you count to five,
and wiggle them on line two!*

Handy Dandy,
Riddledy Roe,
Which hand will you have,
High or low?

*Hide something small in one hand,
and move your hands around,
shifting it from one to another.
Then, holding one hand up high,
the other down low, ask,
"Which hand holds the surprise?"*

Hiccup, hiccup, go away,
Come again another day.
Hiccup, hiccup, when I bake,
I will give you a butter cake.

*If your child has hiccups, say this rhyme
to make her smile.*

Inkey, Winkey, Wonkey,
My dear donkey,
Thank you, thank you,
Inkey, Winkey, Wonkey.

A fun rhyme for reminding children to say thank you!

Through the teeth
And past the gums,
Look out, stomach –
Here it comes!

A useful game to speed up meal times!

One for father,
One for mother,
One for you,
But NOT another.

*A rhyme to encourage sharing –
or eating up the last spoonfuls!*

Not yet three, please listen to me

Between 24 and 36 months

By two years of age your child is no longer a toddler, but a small child. She loves to talk, and talks continually to herself about what she is doing. Her talk reflects her own ideas and opinions, and includes saying "no". Towards the end of her second year she is ready to cooperate in activities with other children and rhymes will encourage this *(Higher than a house, Jack in the box, Sometimes I'm very small)*. By three years there is a breakthrough to fluent talk.

Between 24 and 30 months she really likes to talk. Listen to her and ask questions; otherwise she may be disappointed. She begins to make statements, ask questions and even give commands. Her pronunciation has developed and she can say longer words, some with three syllables. She picks up new rhymes quickly, and proudly joins in with favourite rhymes, saying complete lines by herself. During this period her vocabulary and grammar develop rapidly.

By 30 months she begins to talk in story form, relating what she did, where she went, or what she is going to do. She is capable of using complex grammar to make full sentences. She starts conversations, asking *What's that?* or *Where's...?*, and can answer questions beginning with *Who?* and *Why?* The gap between words she understands and words she can say is getting less. She can say complete rhymes by herself if she is given an opportunity. She laughs at nonsense words and phrases, like *Higglety Pigglety POP,* and has fun repeating them. She even makes up her own series of rhyming nonsense words.

As you say the rhymes, try to:

* keep using a soft voice but gradually quicken your speed.
* take turns with your child saying lines or phrases, until she can say the rhyme by herself.
* let her take over the actions whilst you say the rhyme.
* let her select in the book the rhymes she would like to say, but continue to introduce new and more challenging rhymes.
* let her talk about the illustrations.
* move your finger along the text as you read the rhyme.

I can ride my bicycle,
We bought it at the shop,
When I see the light is red,
I know I have to stop.
When I see the light is green,
I know that I can go.
On the way, every day,
Green means, "Go!"

*A good rhyme to reinforce safety
training – adaptable for use
on the bus or in the car.*

I went along the street one day,
And I saw a CAR across the way,
And what do you think I heard it say?
Vroom, vroom, vroom.

I went along the street one day,
And I saw a POLICE CAR across the way,
And what do you think I heard it say?
Neena-neena.

Sing this with a different vehicle each time
(Bus – Brum, brum, brum, Tractor – Chug, chug, chug, etc.,)
Music – see page 45

Left, right, left, right,
Marching down the street,
Left, right, left, right,
Who will we meet?

Butterfly, butterfly,
Trying to reach the sky,
Why do you flutter by,
Butterfly, butterfly?

Join both hands together to make a butterfly.

Higglety Pigglety POP
The dog has eaten the mop,
The pig's in a hurry,
The cat's in a flurry,
Higglety Pigglety POP!

The turkey is a funny bird,
Its head goes wobble, wobble,
All it knows is just **one word**,
And that is "gobble, gobble".

Under a stone where the earth was firm
I found a wiggly, wriggly worm:
"Good morning," I said.
"How are you, today?"
But the wiggly worm just wriggled away!

*Hide your right index finger inside your left hand.
Let it wriggle out and listen to the conversation,
and then wiggle away.*

Higher than a house,
Higher than a tree,
Oh, whatever can it be?
Can you guess?
No – or yes?

Jack in the box
Sits so still,
"Won't you come out?"
"Yes, I WILL!"

Child crouches down, and jumps up on, "Yes, I WILL!"

Sometimes I'm very small,
Sometimes I'm very tall,
Shut your eyes and turn around,
And guess which I am now.

Child asks someone to guess if he's tall or small.

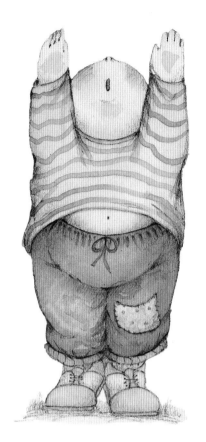

Clap with Mother,
Mother, Mother.
Clap one hand
And then the other.

This little girl is ready for bed,
Down on the sheet, she lays her head,
Wraps herself in covers tight,
This is the way she sleeps all night.

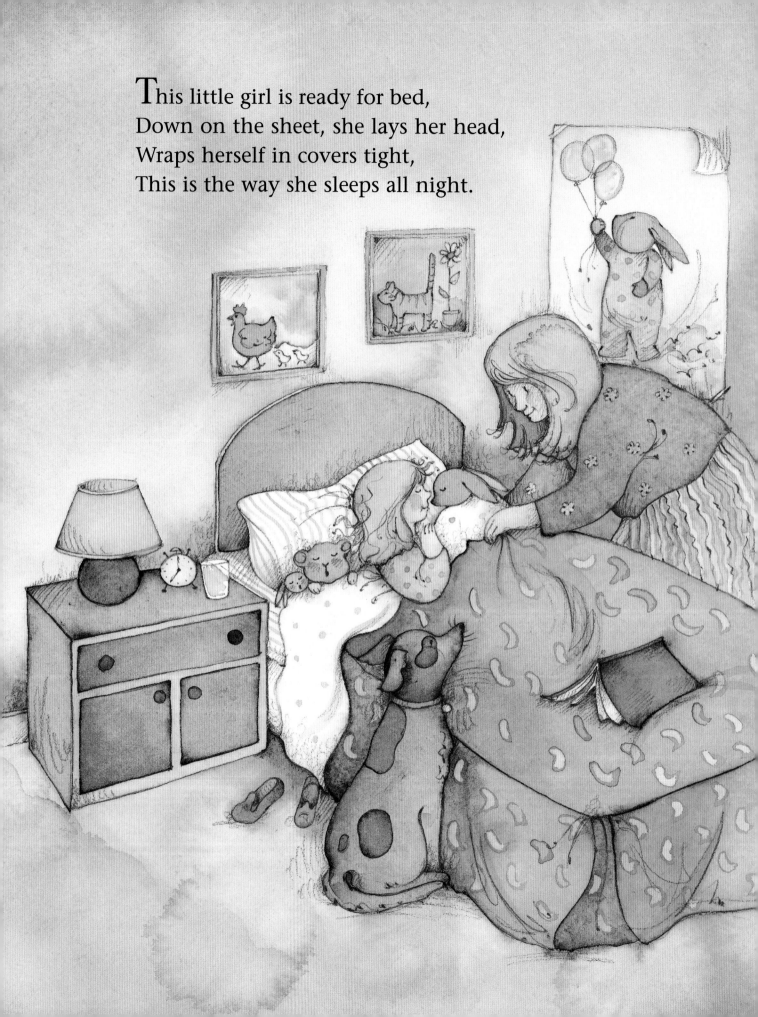

Michael's been a good boy today,
A good boy today,
A good boy today,
Michael shared his toys today –
Well done, Michael!

Music – see page 45

Thank you for the world so sweet,
Thank you for the food we eat,
Thank you for the birds that sing,
Thank you, WORLD, for everything.

Music – see page 45

Music for Rhymes

These rhymes are set to folk melodies, so if you know a different tune, feel free to sing it – or even make up your own!

This is the way

See pages 10 and 28

Sing to the tune of Mulberry Bush

This is the way you splash with your feet, splash with your feet, splash with your feet.

This is the way you splash with your feet. Splish, splash, SPLOSH!

Good night, Mummy

See page 11

Sing to the tune of Good night, ladies!

Good night, Mum - my, Good night, Dad - dy,

Good night, Mi - chael, It's time to say, "Good night!"

Dancing, dancing

See page 25

Dan - cing, dan - cing, jum - ping up and down, Dan - cing, dan - cing,

tur - ning round and round, Dan - cing, dan - cing, fal - ling on the ground.

I went along the street one day

See page 36

I went a - long the street one day, And I saw a car a - cross the way, And

what do you think I heard it say? Vroom, vroom vroom.

Michael's been a good boy today

See page 43

Sing to the tune of Merrily we roll along *(adapted)*

Mi - chael's been a good boy to - day, A good boy to - day, A good boy to - day,

Mi - chael shared his toys to - day — Well done, Mi - chael!

Thank you for the world so sweet

See page 43

This rhyme can also be sung to the English hymn tune Buckland

Thank you for the world so sweet, Thank you for the food we eat,

Thank you for the birds that sing, Thank you, WORLD, for ev' - ry - thing.

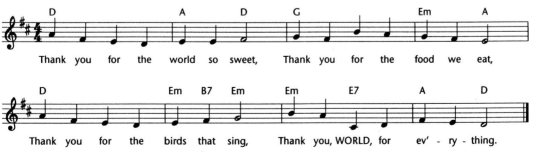

Index of First Lines